Teggs is no ordinary dinosaur –
he's an **ASTROSAUR!** Captain of
the amazing spaceship DSS *Sauropod*, he
goes on dangerous missions and fights
evil – along with his faithful crew,
Gipsy, Arx and Iggy!

Visit the BRAND NEW Astrosaurs
website for games, downloads,
competitions and the chance to
meet the crew and find out your
astrosaur name!
www.astrosaurs.co.uk

Read all the adventures of
Teggs, Gipsy, Arx and Iggy!

BOOK TWO:
THE HATCHING HORROR

Coming soon

BOOK THREE:
THE SEAS OF DOOM

BOOK FOUR:
THE MIND-SWAP MENACE

Find out more at
www.astrosaurs.co.uk

Astrosaurs

RIDDLE OF THE
RAPTORS

Steve Cole

Illustrated by
Charlie Fowkes

RED FOX

RIDDLE OF THE RAPTORS
A RED FOX BOOK 978 0 099 47294 0

First published in Great Britain by Red Fox,
an imprint of Random House Children's Books

This edition published 2005

10

Set in Bembo Schoolbook

Red Fox Books are published by Random House Children's Books,
61–63 Uxbridge Road, London W5 5SA
A RANDOM HOUSE GROUP COMPANY

Addresses for companies within The Random House Group Limited
can be found at: www.randomhouse.co.uk/offices.htm

THE RANDOM HOUSE GROUP Limited Reg. No. 954009
www.kidsatrandomhouse.co.uk

The Random House Group Limited supports The Forest Stewardship Council
(FSC), the leading international forest certification organisation. All our titles that
are printed on Greenpeace approved FSC certified paper carry the FSC logo. Our
paper procurement policy can be found at www.rbooks.co.uk/environment.

Printed and bound in Great Britain by CPI Bookmarque, Croydon, CR0 4TD

A CIP catalogue record for this book is available from the British Library.

For Tobey

WARNING!

THINK YOU KNOW ABOUT DINOSAURS?

THINK AGAIN!

The dinosaurs . . .

Big, stupid, lumbering reptiles. Right?

All they did was eat, sleep and roar a bit. Right?

Died out millions of years ago when a big meteor struck the Earth. Right?

Wrong!

The dinosaurs weren't stupid. They may have had small brains, but they used them well. They had big thoughts and big dreams.

By the time the meteor hit, the last dinosaurs had already left Earth for ever. Some breeds had discovered how to travel through space as early as the Triassic period, and were already enjoying a new life among the stars.

No one has found evidence of dinosaur technology yet. But the first fossil bones were only unearthed in 1822, and new finds are being made all the time. The proof is out there, buried in the ground.

And the dinosaurs live on, way out in space, even now. They've settled down in a place they call the Jurassic Quadrant and over the last sixty-five million years they've gone on evolving . . .

The dinosaurs we'll be meeting are

 part of a special group called the Dinosaur Space Service. These heroic herbivores are not just dinosaurs.

They are *astrosaurs*!

NOTE: The following story has been translated from secret Dinosaur Space Service records. Earthling dinosaur names are used throughout, although some changes have been made for easy reading. There's even a guide to help you pronounce the dinosaur names at the back of the book.

THE CREW OF THE DSS SAUROPOD

**CAPTAIN
TEGGS STEGOSAUR**

ARX ORANO,
FIRST OFFICER

GIPSY SAURINE,
COMMUNICATIONS
OFFICER

IGGY TOOTH,
CHIEF ENGINEER

Jurassic Quadrant

Ankylos

Steggos

Diplox

INDEPEND
DINOSAU
ALLIANC

vegetarian sector

Squawk
Major

DSS
UNION OF
PLANETS

PTEROSAUR

Tri System

Corytho

Lambeos

Cr

Iguanos

Aqua Minor

SEA

OUTER SPACE

Geldos Cluster

Teerex
Major

Olympus

TYRANNOSAUR
TERRITORIES

carnivore

Planet Sixty

Raptos

sector

THEROPOD EMPIRE

Megalos

vegmeat
zone
(neutral space)

LE SPACE

Pliosaur
Nurseries

Not to scale

RIDDLE OF THE RAPTORS

Chapter One

THE ADVENTURE BEGINS

Space. It stretched on for ever.

Distant stars twinkled. Comets showed off their sparkling tails. Strange planets hung like bright bulbs in the black sky.

Teggs Stegosaur stared out at it all in wonder. He was standing on the top deck of a massive space station – the headquarters of the Dinosaur Space Service.

3

At last, he thought. After years of training, I've made it. I'm an *astrosaur*! He frowned. But why have I been asked to come to headquarters alone? I hope I haven't messed up already!

Just then, a small pterosaur flapped noisily down the corridor towards him. "Admiral Rosso will see you now," it squawked. "Follow me! Follow me!"

Teggs gulped, and lumbered after the flying reptile on his four squat, scaly

legs. He was a handsome, orange-brown stegosaurus, eight metres long from the point of his beak to the tip of his spiny tail. A line of armoured plates ran down his scaly back like a dozen small sails.

The pterosaur perched just outside the admiral's office. "In you go," it screeched. "In you go!"

Teggs pushed through the heavy jungle vines that hung down over the doorway. The floor was thick with juicy moss, and the walls were bright with flowers and fruits. Here and there, tall, thick tree trunks stretched up to the high grassy ceiling. Astrosaurs always kept plenty of plants around the place, and not just because they were good to eat. Their spaceships ran on dung, so every meal meant a little more fuel for the engines.

"Ah! Young Teggs!" boomed Admiral Rosso from behind a vast wooden desk.

He was the crusty old barosaurus in charge of the Dinosaur Space Service. "Thank you for coming."

Teggs carefully raised his front legs in a dinosaur salute. "You wanted to see me, sir?"

"I wanted to congratulate you," smiled the admiral. His scaly head bobbed about on a neck as long as a fireman's hose — and ten times thicker. "You have passed your final Space Service tests with a record-breaking score. You are without doubt the bravest, most daring — and *hungriest* astrosaur ever to train here."

Teggs blushed and quickly swallowed the mouthful of ferns he'd pulled from the floor. "Thank you, sir. Er, sorry for eating your office, sir."

"Nothing wrong with a hearty appetite," the admiral chuckled. "But I think it's *adventure* you're truly hungry for."

Teggs grinned.
"My stomach's
rumbling at the
thought of it!"
"That's why I'm
putting you in
charge of your
very own
spaceship," said the
admiral. "I'm making
you a captain!"
"Captain? And my very own
spaceship?" Teggs's beak dropped open
in amazement. This was a dream come
true!

The admiral pulled aside a curtain
of jungle creepers to reveal a window.
Through it, Teggs saw an amazing
spaceship. It was shaped like an
enormous egg, with six thick prongs
sticking out. At the end of every prong
sat a slightly smaller egg. Teggs
supposed these were the shuttles.

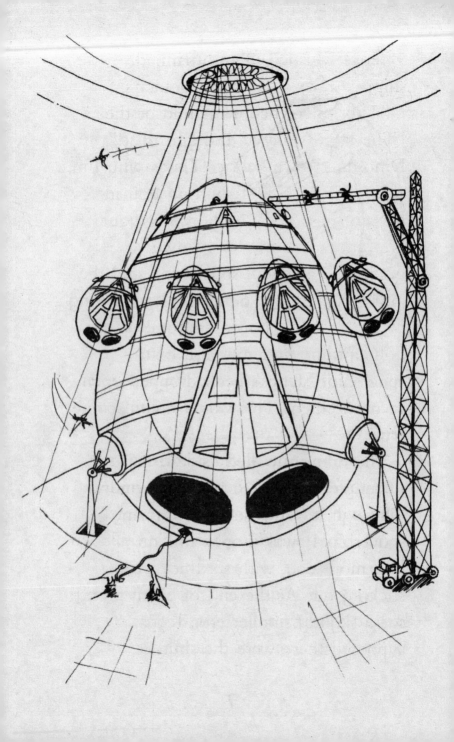

Teggs whistled in wonder. "That's *my* ship?"

"That's her," beamed the admiral. "The DSS *Sauropod*, finest in the entire Dinosaur Space Service. That ship — and you, Captain Teggs — have been chosen for a very important mission." He unrolled some star charts with his long tail. "Recognize this?"

"That's the Jurassic Quadrant," said Teggs. "The part of space we call home." He pointed to one half of it with a tail spike. "Those green planets are in the Vegetarian Sector. The red ones are where the carnivores live."

"Yes, those mean old meat-eaters," said the admiral. "We've all come a long way from dear old Earth. Such a shame that beastly space rock walloped into it."

"Yes, sir." Teggs shuddered. If the dinosaurs hadn't discovered space travel before the meteor hit, they'd all have been wiped out! "Do you think anyone will ever live on Earth again, sir?"

"Who knows?" sighed the admiral. "But we dinosaurs have thrived in outer space. Earth is just a titchy speck compared to the vastness of the Jurassic Quadrant!"

Teggs nodded keenly. "And there's still so much of it to explore!"

"That's where you come in," said the admiral. "You're now a fully trained astrosaur captain. Your mission is to explore space in the DSS *Sauropod*. To go in peace . . . To spread the way of the plant-eater . . . To keep an eye on those greedy meat-eaters . . . And to protect our people, wherever they may be."

Teggs nodded even *more* keenly. "I'll need a crew," he said.

"I've already got you one." The admiral swatted a button on the wall with his tail, and the window turned

into a scanner screen.
It showed a picture of
a green triceratops
with three proud horns
and a parrot-like beak.

"This is Arx Orano,"
said the admiral. "He's
a very well respected
astrosaur. He'll be your first officer."

Teggs smiled. Then the image changed
to show a pretty duck-billed dinosaur,
striped all over.

"This is your communications officer,
Gipsy Saurine," said the admiral. "You
can see from her snout that she's a

hadrosaur. Her
mind's as sharp as
a raptor's claw and
she loves a
challenge." He
smiled. "That's
why I've put her
on *your* ship!"

"I'm glad to have her on board," said Teggs.

The picture changed again. Now it showed a tough looking iguanodon on his hind legs. His arms were thick and strong.

"And this is Iggy Tooth," said the admiral. "A top engineer. He can turn a clawful of scrap into a space motor before you can say 'ornithomimosaur'."

Teggs gulped. He wasn't sure if he could say that at all.

"He's also very good in battle," the admiral said. "So if you ever find trouble – find Iggy fast!"

"I will," said Teggs grimly.

"So, when am I off on these exciting missions?"

"Oh, soon. Very soon." The admiral cleared his throat. "But there's a little something I need you to do first . . ."

Chapter Two

BATTLE STATIONS!

"A taxi service!" huffed Captain Teggs for the hundredth time. "The finest ship in the fleet, the best crew . . . and the admiral turns us into a taxi service!"

Gipsy turned her long, flat snout towards him. "Not just *any* taxi service, Captain," she reminded him. "We're in charge of the Vegetarian Sector's top athletes. We'll get them to the Great Dinosaur Games in style!"

Arx nodded his frilly head. "It's the biggest space sports

contest *ever*. Every race in the quadrant is coming to Olympus for the games. And when those miserable meat-eaters see the DSS *Sauropod* arrive, think how impressed they'll be!"

"I suppose so." Teggs chewed grumpily on some ferns from the wall of his control pit. "How long before we arrive?"

"Right now, we're just passing the moons of Minnos," said Gipsy. "That's the halfway point. Then, once we've swung round Planet Sixty, it's straight on to Olympus. We should arrive tomorrow night."

"The games start the day after!" Arx added.

"And nothing to do until then," sighed Teggs. "I was hoping for a little more action—"

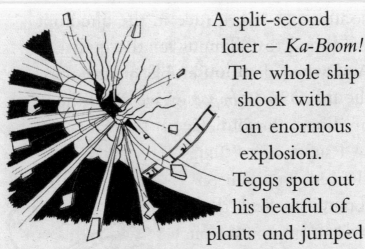

A split-second later – *Ka-Boom!* The whole ship shook with an enormous explosion.

Teggs spat out his beakful of plants and jumped up from the control pit. "What was *that*?" he bellowed.

"Warning! Warning!" The shriek of the alarm pterosaur echoed out from every speaker on the ship. "Unknown invaders coming aboard!"

Arx swung his great head round to his instruments. "Someone's blown a hole in our ship!"

"On our first ever flight?" cried Gipsy. "That's not fair!"

"I wanted action," Teggs muttered.

"And I guess I've got it!"

"Red alert!" The alarm pterosaur squawked even louder. "Raptors on board! Repeat – *raptors on board!*"

"Battle stations!" Teggs roared. "Gipsy, where *are* these raptors?"

"The hole's on level seven, Captain," Gipsy reported. "It's close to the relaxation room." Then the crest of her scaly face flushed bright blue with worry. "Uh-oh. That's where the athletes are!"

"We have to drive these raptors off the ship – *fast*," said Teggs. "Arx, get Iggy on to it!"

Arx jabbed the communicator with his nose horn. "Iggy!" he snapped. "Raptor invaders on level seven. Our athletes are in danger. Prepare for battle!"

"Switch on the scanners, Gipsy," Teggs ordered.

At first they could only see the rocky

moons of Minnos. Then
a sinister craft came
into view, hanging in
space like a giant
ivory tooth.

"A raptor death-
ship!" cried Gipsy.
"We've flown into
an ambush!"

Suddenly another
big explosion sent the
Sauropod spinning. Teggs's
seven-ton body was rolled over and over
until he smashed into the thick plant-
life that covered the nearest wall. His
team of tiny flying reptiles – fifty daring
dimorphodon – flapped wildly about
the flight deck, trying to sort out the
damage. They bashed the controls with
their beaks and yanked on levers with
tough, bony claws.

Arx rose from the grassy floor and
checked his instruments. "There are *five*

death-ships out there! They were hiding behind the moons. Now we're surrounded!"

"Put up the shields!" Teggs yelled. "And fetch me my armour!"

The dimorphodon crew rushed to obey. In moments, three of the flapping reptiles were fitting Teggs into his head and tail armour. "I'll join the fight with Iggy down below," he said. "Arx, Gipsy, try to get us out of here."

"Understood, Captain," barked Arx. The dimorphodon team leaders flapped down to perch on his head, ready to take his commands.

Gipsy looked at Teggs. "Be careful, sir," she said.

★

As the moss-lined lift heaved down to the crew decks, Teggs heard the sound of fighting grow louder. As the lift reached the seventh floor, he gritted his teeth. The spines that ran along his arched back turned a deep, warning red.

"I'll get those raptors," he muttered fiercely. "They'll be sorry they stepped onto *my* ship!"

As the doors opened Teggs sprang out, flexed the great, spiked club of his armoured tail, then charged along the corridor.

He found the battle raging ahead of him. The air was thick with shrieks and roars. Nimble velociraptors in full battle armour skipped around the heavier ankylosaurs blocking their way. A dozen iguanodon reared up on their hind legs, roaring. Their claws ended in metal tips that fired stun rays into the raptor ranks. The beams of light bounced off the raptors' chestplates and helmets. Teggs's ears rang with *thwacks* and *thuds* as his crew's heavy tails swiped through the air at their attackers.

Iggy Tooth was in the thick of the fighting. He caught sight of Teggs and swiftly saluted. "Set your stun claws to maximum, boys!" he cried, a blur of green scales as he dodged his way through the fighting, keeping perfect balance with his short, stiff tail. "The captain's come to join us! We can't lose now!"

But even as he spoke, two raptors finally managed to tear their way straight past the massive ankylosaur that barred their way. They bared their blood-red teeth at Teggs.

"Sssurrender your ship, Captain," hissed the largest of the two raptors as they advanced with razor-sharp claws. "Or you shall die!"

Chapter Three

KIDNAP!

Teggs shook his head and sneered at the approaching raptors. "I'm not ready to become a stego-burger just yet," he growled. "And it'll take more than a couple of corny carnivores like you to take my ship!"

With that, Teggs lashed out with his armoured tail and sent the first raptor flying. The second brought its jaws down hard on the spiky, bone-like club at the tail's end.

It was a bad move. A second later, every tooth in its ugly head was broken and tinkling down to the mossy floor.

The furious carnivore gnashed its gums and turned to its fallen mate. "Ssstop him!"

The first raptor leaped forward once more to bite Teggs on the neck. Teggs quickly ducked down and turned with surprising speed, so that his attacker smacked into his back. The raptor toppled backwards and landed on top of its friend.

Teggs prepared to fight his way

through to Iggy. But then a strange wailing noise started up. At once, the raptors broke off from the battle and backed off.

"You hear that, boys?" cried Iggy triumphantly. "That's the raptor retreat signal! They're giving up! Come on, let's see them off the ship!"

As Iggy's battle squad charged off after the retreating raptors, Teggs pressed his head up against the communicator. "Captain to flight deck. Well done, crew. We've scared them off! The raptors are running away!"

But Arx sounded worried. "I don't think we *did* scare them off, Captain," he said. "We only fired off two laser bolts, and the raptor ships didn't even fire back."

Teggs thought hard. "You know, you might be right," he said slowly. "Those soldiers gave up pretty easily too. One minute they wanted me to surrender the *Sauropod* – the next they were retreating back to their ship as fast as their claws would carry them."

Gipsy's voice sounded over the speaker. "Perhaps they only retreated because they'd got what they came for . . ."

"Of course!" Teggs grunted and charged off down the corridor after Iggy. The raptors didn't really want to take the ship at all. They started the fight just to keep Teggs and his crew busy – while they went after the athletes . . .

"They must be planning to ruin the Great Dinosaur Games!" he cried. "But surely they wouldn't *dare* eat our greatest athletes!"

Teggs charged into the *Sauropod's* enormous relaxation room. It was like a miniature forest, with a crystal clear bathing pool in its centre. Ordinarily the dinosaur athletes would've been chewing and resting or splashing about. But right now they were all cowering behind a large saltasaurus wrestler in the corner.

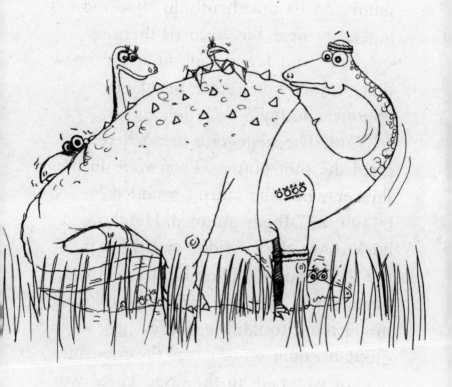

"Are they gone?" whimpered a maiasaura shot-putter, its belly pressed low against the grass so that it could barely be seen.

"Yes, they've gone back to their ship," said Teggs. "I was worried they'd taken all of you with them!"

"No way," said the saltasaurus, the bumps on its hide bristling. "Two raptors looked in here, but I scared them off."

"I see," said Teggs doubtfully. He knew that raptors didn't scare easily. "Is anyone missing?"

"Wait! The stegoceras aren't here," cried the shot-putter. "They were in the shower when the alarms sounded."

"Oh no!" Teggs groaned. He charged back down the corridor and through the shower doors. Then he stuck his head inside. "Anyone there?" he asked as he peered through the steam.

But his only answer was the mournful drip of water on to the floor. There was no sign of the stegoceras athletes. The showers were empty.

Teggs stomped back to the communicator in the wall. "Captain to flight deck," he growled. "You were right, Arx. This wasn't just a raid. It was a *kidnapping!*"

Chapter Four

A DEADLY MESSAGE

Captain Teggs sat tensely in his control pit, chewing on twigs.

Arx had found images of the two stegoceras and Gipsy had put them on the scanner. The athletes were perky orange creatures, each about the size of a goat. One was named Hank, the other Crank. They had feeble forearms, long, straight tails and ran about on two legs. But their heads were truly eye-catching: a solid lump of bone the size of a football bulged above their snouts.

"What sport do they play?" wondered Gipsy.

"They were hot tips to win the head-butting contest," Arx said.

"I'm an idiot!" sighed Teggs. "Two days to go until the Great Dinosaur Games, and I let a bunch of raptors sneak on board and take our best butters. I must have a brain the size of a ping-pong ball!"

Arx cleared his throat. "Er, you *do* have a brain the size of a ping-pong ball, Captain," he said delicately. "You know, being a stegosaurus and all."

"So I do!" said Teggs, cheering up a bit. "I shouldn't be so hard on myself."

Just then, Teggs's personal communicator beeped.

"Uh-oh," he said. "Here's someone who *will* be hard on me. It's Admiral Rosso!"

"Captain Teggs!" boomed Admiral Rosso. "I've read your report. I can hardly believe what has happened. It's a disaster! A mess! A total foul-up!"

"I'm sorry, sir," said Teggs. "Perhaps . . . perhaps I'm just not good enough to be captain of the *Sauropod*."

"Piffle," said the admiral sternly. "Everyone makes mistakes, Captain. It's how you make up for them that counts." He paused. "Just make sure you sort out *this* mistake fast – before the Great Dinosaur Games begin!"

The communicator switched off.

"Are you all right, Captain?" asked Arx gently.

"Never mind me," said Teggs. "It's those poor stegoceras athletes I'm worried about!"

Gipsy raised her snout in the air and whistled and hooted at the dimorphodon flight crew. A few of them flapped down at once and massaged their captain's spiky back with their claws. "So, what do we do now?" she asked.

Iggy was pacing up and down the

flight deck in a foul temper, clicking his thumb spikes. "I say we hunt down these velociraptor vermin and *make* them give us back our athletes!"

"The Jurassic Quadrant is a big area to search," Arx reminded him.

"Why did they only take the head-butters out of everyone on board?" wondered Gipsy.

"You've got something there!" Teggs rose up suddenly, and the dimorphodon flapped off in fright. "The raptors looked in the athletes' room, but kept searching till they found the stegoceras in the showers. Why?"

"Well, if the raptors *have* taken the stegoceras for a reason," Arx said, "we can only wait and see if they tell us what it is."

There was a sudden creaking, squeaking noise from Gipsy's communications console. "I'm getting a message, Captain. Picture and sound," she reported briskly, checking the readout. "It's from a raptor!"

"Put it on the scanner," Teggs ordered.

The screen showed the hateful features of a big, scaly raptor. Clearly it had been in many battles over the

years. Its pointed jaw was scuffed and
scraped, and it wore a black eye-patch
over one eye.

"I am General Loki," said the raptor
in a silky smooth whisper. "Commander
of the Seven Fleets of Death! Ruler
of the meat mines of Raptos! Eater of
edmontosaurus, devourer of
diplodocus—"

"And all-round pain in the tail," Teggs

cut in before the raptor got really carried away. He had heard of General Loki — the nastiest, meanest velociraptor in the Jurassic Quadrant. "At least you've got less of a lisp than your raptor crew. What do you want?"

Loki narrowed his one remaining eye. "It's what *you* want that we should be discussing, Captain Teggs . . ." Loki moved aside from the scanner cameras to reveal the two stegoceras athletes hunched up behind him. Both of them had grubby bandages wrapped round their heads.

"Hank! Crank!" Teggs reared up out

of his control pit. "Are you OK?"

"We're cool!" Hank and Crank chorused, and lightly tapped their heads together as if to prove it. "Ouch!" they both yelled.

Gipsy frowned. "Have the raptors hurt you?"

"Nah," said Hank. "We just woke up with a headache." He waved his feeble forearm at his bandage. "Look! Some raptor doctors checked us out, then gave us these headbands!"

Crank nodded enthusiastically. "Cool or what!"

The stegoceras were about to bash heads again when two raptor guards restrained them.

Loki came back into view. "So you see, Captain," he said. "Your athletes are fit and well. And they'll stay that way if you agree to our terms."

Teggs glared at him. "And just what exactly *are* your terms?"

"You must pay us a billion pieces of purest gold!" Loki laughed nastily. "And if you refuse, *your* athletes become *my* supper!"

Chapter Five

SHOWDOWN ON PLANET SIXTY

Iggy, Arx, Teggs and Gipsy stared at each other in disbelief.

"A billion pieces?" Teggs spluttered. "You're crazy! It would take *years* to gather all that gold!"

"Oh. Really?" Loki looked a little downcast, and clicked his claws. "All right then . . . call it twenty."

"Twenty?" echoed Teggs.

Loki nodded. "But throw in a nice flat-screen satellite monitor too. Mine's just broken."

Iggy, Arx, Teggs and Gipsy stared at each other once again, in still *deeper* disbelief.

"From a billion pieces . . . to twenty?" Teggs started counting on his toes, then frowned. "That *is* quite a drop – isn't it?"

"Raptors are totally rubbish at doing deals, Captain," Arx said in a low voice. "They normally sort out any squabbles by biting each other."

"Mind you," said Iggy grudgingly, "that Loki's smarter than he looks. Those flat-screen satellite monitors are brilliant!"

"Oh, and we want some moss too,"

Loki added as if the thought had just occurred to him. "It goes so well with raw apatosaurus." He licked his leathery lips with a forked tongue. "The exchange will be made at noon tomorrow on Planet Sixty."

Teggs frowned. "Planet Sixty? Isn't that on the way to Olympus?"

"Yes, Captain," said Arx. "It's a small, swampy planet just outside the Vegetarian Sector. It's so dull, no one could be bothered to name it!"

Loki smiled. "I trust your . . . *flimsy* new ship can reach Planet Sixty in time?"

Teggs narrowed his eyes. "We'll be there."

"Splendid. But no tricks," said the grizzled general. "You're to come unarmed, Captain, with just one member of your crew. Until tomorrow . . ." He nodded his head in farewell, and the screen went blank.

"What do we do, Captain?" asked Gipsy.

"What *can* we do?" Teggs uprooted a fern from the floor and chewed it grumpily. "You heard the admiral. We need to sort this out fast. Next stop, Planet Sixty – full speed ahead!"

And so the *Sauropod* sailed through space towards the pick-up point.

"Planet Sixty is coming into range, Captain," announced Gipsy at last. She blinked her wide eyes at him. "Iggy says the shuttle is ready to depart."

Teggs came out of the control pit. "Those raptors are up to something," he said. "I feel it in my tail spikes."

As he stomped off towards the shuttle, Teggs had an uneasy feeling that something was badly wrong. He felt naked without his electro-tail armour. He bet Iggy felt the same without his stun claws. But Loki had insisted they must come unarmed. Teggs couldn't risk crossing him while the two athletes were prisoners.

Even so – would the raptors keep their side of the bargain?

Iggy saluted Teggs as he came aboard the shuttle. "Dung burners set

43

to maximum, Captain!"

"OK," Teggs nodded. "Blast off!"

The shuttle – shaped like a giant egg with two noisy motors on the fat end – began to shudder and shake as the power began to build. The engines ignited. Soon, the sweet smell of dinosaur manure filled the air as the 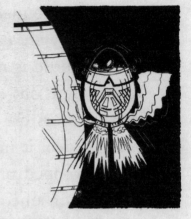 shuttle thundered away into space.

Within minutes they were flying through the grotty green skies of Planet Sixty. With a slithering bump and a rattling roar, the shuttle skidded to a stop on the swampy surface.

Teggs opened the doors and led the way outside. Iggy waddled close behind him carrying the ransom on his back.

They hadn't walked far before they saw the raptor death shuttle – an enormous, pointed spike with a blood-red tip. Next to it stood General Loki and three of his raptor guards, watching over the athletes with

hungry eyes.

"Welcome, Captain," sneered Loki. He eyed the bundle on Iggy's back. "You have met my demands, I see."

"Let's just get this over with," said Teggs. He swished his enormous tail from side to side menacingly. "Give us back our athletes!"

With a hiss, the raptor guards herded the stegoceras over to Teggs. One of the guards came towards Iggy, its claws raised and ready to slash. It cut clean through the thick twine that bound the ransom bundle to the iguanodon's back and paraded the package back to its ship in triumph.

Teggs peered at the athletes with their bandaged heads. "You two OK?"

"We're cool," said Hank.

"Just glad to be out of that fleapit," added Crank, nodding at the raptor shuttle.

"Farewell, Captain!" called Loki. "Enjoy the Great Dinosaur Games! I'm sure they'll go with a bang!" With a nasty chuckle, he scuttled into his ship, which took off at once.

"Good riddance!" yelled Crank.

"Totally," Hank nodded. "That ship stank of meat, man!" He tried to mime being suffocated, but his little forearms couldn't reach his neck.

"Wait a second," Iggy said gruffly. His nostrils were twitching. "Did either

of you *sit* in any of
that meat?"

Hank and Crank
shook their bandaged
heads.

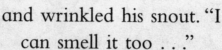

Teggs sniffed the air,
and wrinkled his snout. "I
can smell it too . . ."

Suddenly the swampy
ground began to shake.
"What's that?" Hank
squeaked.

"Something big," shouted
Iggy, looking around as the pounding
on the ground got louder. "Coming
this way!"

Teggs lumbered up a small hill to see
what it was – and froze in his tracks.

A terrifying creature was bounding
up towards him – a real giant, at least
three times the size of Teggs. It stood
upright on powerful legs as big as tree
trunks. Its massive mouth brimmed

with dagger-like teeth. Hot on its scaly heels, another ten of the monsters were approaching fast.

"Back to the ship, quick!" called Teggs as he thundered back down the hill. "*There are T. rexes on this planet!*"

Chapter Six

DANGEROUS FLIGHT

Teggs led the charge back to the shuttle.
The ground shook like it was going to
open up beneath their feet.

T. rexes didn't normally hunt in packs –
unless they were scouting out new
planets to take over . . .

"You're welcome to this dump,"
muttered Teggs. Then he skidded to a
halt. Iggy and the others almost
crashed into him.

Another T. rex, the biggest yet, was
looming over their shuttle.

Teggs squared up to the ferocious
carnivore. "Iggy, I'll lead it off. Get
those athletes inside the ship!"

Iggy hesitated. "But, Captain—"
"Do it!" growled Teggs.

He ran to the edge of a cliff, and the
T. rex chased after him. Then Teggs
faced up to the monster. He swung his
tail around so fast that the spikes on
the end of it became an ivory blur.

The terrifying tyrannosaur roared
and lunged forward, but Teggs's
tail whacked it on the side
of its head. Staggering
sideways in surprise,
the T. rex fell over
the edge of the
cliff and into the
swamp below.

But there was no
time to celebrate.
Teggs rushed
back to the
shuttle to find
the whole
snarling gang

of T. rexes were now blocking his way.

"This *our* planet," growled their
leader. "You in big trouble, plant-boy."

"We were just visiting," Teggs told
her. "We'll be off now. Leave you to it."

The T. rex shook its head. "No."

"Er, can't we talk about this?" asked
Teggs hopefully, edging towards the
shuttle.

"No," it said.

Teggs suddenly remembered what his
astrosaur trainer had taught him:

T. rexes hate talking. They've never learned how to do it properly. Ten seconds into a conversation and they usually eat the person they're speaking to.

"We HUNGRY!" roared the T. rex leader. It opened its jaws and lunged at Teggs. He rolled clear just in time — and the creature crunched down on one of the shuttle's motors. Its teeth tore the engine clear off!

"Take off, Iggy!" yelled Teggs. "Never

mind me! With only one engine you'll have a bumpy ride, but you might just make it!"

The T. rex leader roared in anger. The engine was jammed in its mouth! It lumbered towards Teggs and tried to stamp on his tail.

Teggs backed away. "Missed me, loser!" he called bravely. But deep down he knew there was no hope of escape. Already the other tyrannosaurs were drawing closer, roaring and snapping their gruesome jaws . . .

The shuttle still hadn't taken off. Teggs guessed Iggy couldn't bring himself to leave his captain behind.

"Go *now*, Iggy!" he yelled. "That's an order!"

"Aye-aye, Captain," said Iggy sadly.

The shuttle's remaining engine burst into life – and made a *very* rude noise. The T. rexes all turned round in shock.

While they were distracted, Teggs pushed past them. The shuttle doors heaved open and he leaped inside, scattering the stegoceras like scaly skittles.

"Welcome back, Captain!" beamed Iggy.

"You didn't make that dreadful noise, did you?" gasped Teggs, warily sniffing the air.

"Not me!" said Iggy, revving the engine. "There must have been a build-up of dung gas trapped in the exhaust pipe. It's clear now."

Teggs sighed. "If only *we* were clear of these T. rexes . . ."

The shuttle took off wonkily. It was meant to fly with two engines, not one. Unbalanced, it started to spin in all directions.

"Cool!" yelled Hank and Crank happily, as if it was a fairground ride. The shuttle bumped and bounced against the ground, and soon the ship's floor was flooded with swamp muck.

"I can't control it!" Iggy shouted.

To Teggs's dismay, the T. rexes were running after the spinning shuttle.

"They're catching up!" yelled Crank.

The T. rexes loomed up, gnashing their jaws in triumph – all except their leader, who still had a mouthful of engine. The shuttle made another rude  noise as it dipped down again.

"I know how you feel," muttered Teggs.

Then, suddenly, his little brain was filled with a big idea.

"There's just one chance," Teggs cried.

He scavenged through the swamp muck until he found a big, sharp stone. "Try to hold her steady, Iggy!" he yelled. Then he picked up the stone with his beak and tossed it in the air.

With a noise like a whip crack his tail lashed out and struck the stone, sending it flying out through the shuttle's doors.

The stone smacked against the engine caught in the T. rex leader's teeth. With a fiery bang, the engine exploded!

The T. rex fell backwards with an angry roar of pain. And to everyone's amazement, the other T. rexes toppled over too!

Iggy hooted for joy. "What happened, Captain? What did you do?"

"The rude noise reminded me – our engines run on gas made by burning dung," said Teggs. "They're full to bursting with it! And that gas is explosive stuff . . ."

"It sure is!" Iggy grinned. "There's a lot to be said for a good, healthy vegetarian's diet!"

Hank and Crank clapped their tiny hands together. "Awesome!" Hank laughed. "The fumes alone were enough to knock those uglies out cold!" Crank added.

Just then, the shuttle's crazy course smoothed out. Iggy beamed at the others. "You know what? I think I'm learning to fly this thing with one engine!"

"Oh!" Hank looked crestfallen. "Can't you go back to shaking us round and nearly crashing like before? That was the *best*!"

Teggs frowned. "You've had one knock on the head too many, Hank!"

The others all laughed, but Teggs had to force a smile. He felt strangely tense

from tail to toes. Why? The danger was
all over now . . .

Wasn't it?

On board the raptor shuttle, General
Loki was rubbing his hands with
glee. "Everything went
exactly as planned!"
he chuckled. "That
idiot Teggs has no
idea what we're
really up to . . ."

"Excuse me, your
horriblenessss," rasped
one raptor warrior.
"We have just detected
T. rexes on Planet Sssixty."

"T. rexes?" Loki's single eye narrowed.
"Why didn't you check before? Those
brutes could have eaten the lot of us!"
He swiped at the warrior, who yelped
and fell to the floor. "Did that stupid
stegosaurus get away safely?"

The raptor nodded quickly. "By the ssskin of his teeth."

"Good," said Loki. "I should hate for anything to happen to Captain Teggs." He chuckled nastily. "At least, not until he's done what we need him to do!"

Chapter Seven

MYSTERY

When it was learned that Captain Teggs had rescued the stegoceras athletes, there were celebrations all over the *Sauropod*.

The other athletes staged a big welcome back party for Hank and Crank.

Admiral Rosso sent special congratulations to the crew – "I knew you could do it!" he beamed.

The grateful organizers of the Great Dinosaur Games even offered Teggs and a guest two special seats in the royal paddock.

On the flight deck, Teggs was still glowing with pride. Soon he would be mingling with royalty! The kings and queens of every dinosaur race would be watching the games. This was the first time they had all gathered together in one place. It was a truly special occasion.

Then Teggs was jolted from his thoughts by a sudden clattering and whistling from the flock of flying reptiles around him.

"We're now in orbit around Olympus, Captain," Gipsy translated.

"I think the dimorphodon are as excited as we are!" She cleared her throat. "Er . . . have you decided who you're taking to the games?"

"Yes . . ." Teggs beamed at the stripy hadrosaur. "You! We'll take a shuttle down to the stadium with the other athletes in about one hour's time."

Gipsy grinned. "Yes, sir." But Teggs's good mood vanished when he saw Arx plodding over, shaking his horned head with worry.

"I've been studying all the data on our recent raptor adventures," said the triceratops. "And something's worrying me."

But before he could go on, the flight deck doors swept open to reveal Hank and Crank. Iggy stood proudly behind them.

"Welcome to the flight deck," said Teggs politely.

"We just realized, we never thanked you properly for paying the ransom to get us back," said Crank. "I bet it was a total fortune, right?"

Teggs and Arx swapped awkward looks.

"Er . . ." Teggs began, "*kind* of . . ."

"That's weird," said Gipsy suddenly. "I'm picking up a strange signal. It's interfering with our communicators."

"Find out where the signal's coming from," Teggs ordered, instantly alert.

"Wow, a captain's work is never done, huh?" grinned Hank. "Sorry to bug you when you're busy. We'll catch you later at the games."

"Yeah!" said Crank. "We're going to crack some serious skull down there, Captain – just for you!"

With that, the stegoceras athletes left the flight deck.

"Good lads," said Iggy quietly. "They'll do us herbivores proud!"

"That's funny, Captain," Gipsy reported. "The interference is clearing now. Just sort of fading away."

"Don't worry, Gipsy," said Teggs. "I'm sure it's probably nothing." He turned back to his first officer. "Now, what were you saying?"

"Listen, Captain," Arx said. "I checked the records for all recent raptor ransom demands. General Loki's demand for twenty gold pieces, a satellite monitor and some moss

65

is actually the *lowest* ransom ever recorded."

"That monitor *was* a beauty, though," Iggy reminded them glumly.

Arx ignored him. "And remember when they got on board? They could've taken *all* the athletes. Why just take Hank and Crank?"

Teggs nodded slowly. "And if it was really money they were after, why not just steal it from the ship?"

"Why not indeed," said Arx. "Those raptors had us at their mercy – but they just gave up and flew away."

"What about those T. rexes on Planet Sixty?" Iggy argued. "I bet Loki knew they were down there. He was leading us into a trap."

"I don't think so," said Arx. "The raptors and T. rexes are fierce enemies."

Gipsy frowned. "Hang on, why did he pick Planet Sixty at all? It's light years away from the raptors' world."

"But very handy for us," said Arx, his horns glinting in the light. "It's on our way to the Dinosaur Games."

"That's crazy!" cried Iggy. "Why would the raptors want to make things easy for us?"

"There can only be one answer," said Teggs impressively.

Everyone looked at him.

Teggs swallowed nervously in the sudden spotlight. "Er . . . Because they *wanted* us to pick up the stegoceras athletes with no delays. They wanted us to get them to the games on time – whatever it took!"

Arx nodded. "I think you're right."

The dimorphodon flight crew clapped their leathery wings politely.

Iggy raised his voice over the applause. "Well, I don't know what they were planning, but security at the games is too tight for any funny business. You can't sneak a single stalk of celery in there without the security guards knowing about it." He sighed. "I should know, I've tried it!"

"Maybe so," said Teggs, turning to Gipsy. "But I think it's time we checked out the raptors' enclosure on Olympus. We've got plenty of questions. Now it's time to get the answers!"

Chapter Eight

RUMBLING THE RAPTORS

Teggs and Gipsy took a shuttle down
to the planet's surface at top speed,
while Arx and Iggy stayed on board
the *Sauropod*.

"No sign of any raptor death ships
in orbit," Arx's voice crackled from the
communicator. "But the *Sauropod* is
getting plenty of admiring looks from
the other ships parked here!"

"So she should," grinned Teggs. "Keep
an eye on things. Gipsy and I are
going to head straight for the raptor
enclosure."

"Good luck, sir," said Arx.

★

Teggs and Gipsy's royal passes got
them swiftly through the crowds. No
one dared to question where the two
dinosaurs were going, and they soon
reached the raptor enclosure.

This was where the raptors trained
for the games. The rough floor was
covered with bones and dark scraps.
Teggs didn't want to examine them too
closely. The whole place was sticky and
shadowy, and it stank of raw meat.

"Quiet, isn't it?" Gipsy hissed.

"Too quiet," Teggs murmured uneasily. He hadn't expected to breeze straight to the heart of the raptors' den. They should have met *some* kind of obstacle by now!

Teggs crept on down the corridors as quietly as a seven-ton animal *can* creep. He thought longingly of the golden seats waiting for them in the royal paddock, glinting in the warm light from the planet's six suns. But a niggling feeling in his heavy bones told him that something bad was going to happen very soon – and that they didn't have long to stop it.

Teggs came to a sudden halt. He'd heard something up ahead – a distant buzzing sound. At first it sounded like a swarm of bees, but then he realized it was the sound of a mighty audience clapping and cheering over TV speakers.

Shuffling forwards, Teggs poked his head round the nearest open door, marked CENTRAL CONTROL. It was a large room with dark TV screens piled up along one wall. A raptor, wearing the peaked cap of a security guard, sat alone in a chair with its back to the screens. Its eyes were glued to a broadcast of the games' opening ceremony on a large monitor.

Teggs cleared his throat. "What do you think you're doing, you snivelling security guard?" he yelled.

The raptor leaped in the air like it had sat on a spike. "Just checking the ssstegocerasss were in position, sssir!" it hissed hurriedly.

"Oh yes?" Teggs frowned at the raptor. "In position for what?"

But the raptor had realized it was *not* explaining itself to its boss, but to some stupid herbivore! "You'll never know," it rasped. Eyes narrowed, it scuttled forwards and threw itself at Teggs's neck.

Luckily, Teggs ducked out of reach just in time. The raptor sailed out through the doorway and into the wall opposite. Gipsy jabbed the back of its

neck with her big bill. The raptor
collapsed, and she sat on it.

"Help!" it shrieked. "I can't move!"

"Answer the captain's questions and
I'll sit somewhere else," said Gipsy
sweetly.

"First question," said Teggs. "Where
are all your raptor buddies?"

"Where it is sssafe," said the raptor
smugly. Then it seemed to think it had
said too much. "I mean – they are all
out training, of courssse."

"Leaving only someone as dumb as
you behind?" Teggs shook his head. "I

don't think so. You raptors are up to something. You're working for General Loki, aren't you?"

"No way!" squealed the raptor. "I have never heard the name of our glorioussly evil Commander of the Ssseven Fleetsss of Death, ruler of the meat mines of Raptosss, eater of edmontosssaurusss and devourer of . . . er . . . ever before in my life. Ever."

Teggs and Gipsy looked doubtfully at each other.

"Fibber," said Teggs.

The raptor gasped. "How did you know?"

Teggs smiled. "That satellite monitor you were watching. It's the one we gave you in return for Hank and Crank!"

"So what have you done to them?" said Gipsy. "Come on, talk –

or I'll jab you where it *really* hurts!"

"Don't, please!" yelped the guard. "I'm the only raptor left on the whole planet. Olympusss is doomed — thanks to your knuckle-headed friends!"

Teggs felt a shiver down his backbone. "What do you mean?"

"I mean," hissed the raptor nastily, "that when we kidnapped your athletesss, our doctors sssecretly placed a big bomb in their ssstupid skulls!"

"What?" gasped Gipsy.

The raptor nodded proudly. "When they bang their heads together hard enough, the bombs will go off — and the royal families of every dinosssaur race will be destroyed in a huge explosion!"

Teggs glared down at their prisoner. "You wouldn't dare! The whole quadrant would come after you for revenge!"

"But firssst there will be chaos," the

raptor hissed. "While every dinosssaur weeps in shock, our battle fleet shall attack their worlds."

Gipsy swallowed hard. "Taken by surprise, they won't stand a chance!"

The raptor laughed. "General Loki shall rule over half the galaxy!" It stared up at Teggs, eyes gleaming under the peak of its cap. "And it's all down to *you*, Captain! By bringing those head-butters here, *you've* helped it to happen!"

Chapter Nine

COUNTDOWN TO CARNAGE

"You're bluffing," Teggs decided. "Why should we believe you?"

"Captain," gasped Gipsy, her crest turning bright blue in alarm. "Remember that strange signal I picked up on the flight deck?"

Teggs nodded. "Sure."

"The signal started when Hank and Crank entered the flight deck, and stopped again when they left!" she said. "Don't you see? Those head bombs must've caused it!"

"We're in trouble," Teggs groaned.

The raptor chuckled. Gipsy jabbed her bill against the back of his head again and he fell silent.

Teggs turned up the volume on the satellite monitor. The commentator speaking was a brachiosaurus with a neck so long he could oversee the entire sprawling stadium.

"*For the first time in fifty years, the royal families of every dinosaur race have been brought together,*" he said seriously. "*A spirit of friendly competition fills the air. Plant eaters and carnivores stand side by side in perfect peace. Of course, that big wire fence between them helps . . .*"

"How long before the games begin?" asked Gipsy.

"*It's almost three o'clock — almost time for the first event*," said the commentator, as if he'd heard her question. "*That's the head-banging contest — also known as the Battle of the Butts . . .*"

"We've got so little time!" squealed Gipsy. "What can we do?"

"Hang on," said Teggs grimly. He began to nose about the raptors' security room. "I'll bet it's round here somewhere . . . aha!" he cried, shoving his head in a cupboard. "Just what's needed!"

"What have you found?" Gipsy asked breathlessly. "A way to defuse the bombs?"

"Nope — moss! It was part of the ransom, remember?" beamed Teggs. He pulled a massive green mouthful out of the cupboard. "I always think better on a full stomach." With that, he scoffed the lot and let out an enormous, satisfied belch. "Now, come on, Gipsy. No more dawdling – we've got a planet to save!"

Back on the *Sauropod*, high above the planet, Arx and Iggy were watching the countdown to the games on the scanner screen. Graceful pterodactyls soared through the air above the

stadium with cameras in their long jaws. They were beaming all the action live to a hundred worlds throughout the dinosaur empire.

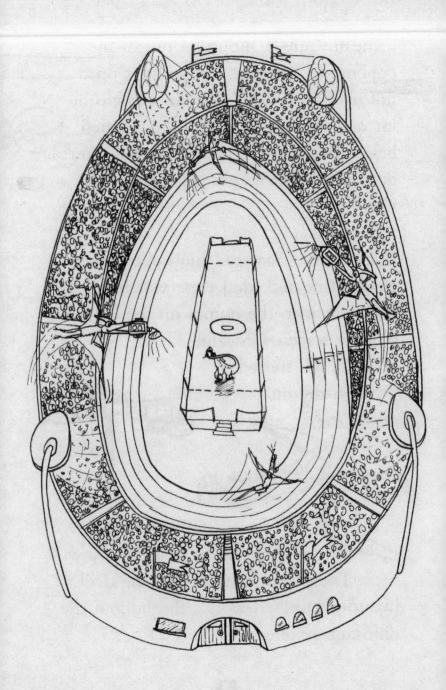

"Look," said Iggy, "Hank and Crank are first up to compete!"

"*And here are two true head-banging heroes,*" said the commentator, "*two plucky stegoceras with the hardest heads of any herbivore around . . . Hank and Crank!*"

The stadium, crammed with thousands of excited dinosaurs, shuddered with a giant roar of approval. Even the dimorphodon flight crew on the *Sauropod* stopped work for a while, watching attentively from perches all about the flight deck.

One pterodactyl zoomed in to show Hank and Crank circling each other on all fours, heads lowered . . .

"*Not long to go now, folks,*" came the commentator's voice. "*When the stadium clock strikes three times, the contest will begin. And I think we're in for some really explosive action today!*"

Teggs and Gipsy raced for the royal paddock. They knew they had to warn the kings and queens and cancel the contest.

They bundled down a long escalator lined with regal red carpet. Then, breathless, they approached the diamond-studded doors that led to the royal paddock.

Suddenly, five stubby-headed carnotaurus stewards appeared from nowhere, blocking the way. The stewards' tiny eyes glinted beneath the short, pointed horns on their eyelids.

"Can we help you?" asked one coldly.

"Even better," said another, "can we *eat* you?"

Teggs ignored him. "We need to get into the royal paddock," he panted.

"Oh yeah?" The first carnotaurus wrinkled its nostrils. "You don't look like royalty to me."

"We have special passes," said Teggs. "Gipsy?"

The colour drained from Gipsy's crest as she searched for them. "I've lost them!"

The stewards laughed, their tiny little forearms waggling with mirth. "You must think we hatched yesterday!" they cried.

Teggs glared at them and turned back to Gipsy. "You must have

dropped them in the raptor enclosure.
You know, when you sat on that
security guard . . ."

He trailed off. The stewards had
narrowed their eyes still further.

"What were a couple of royal
herbivores doing inside a raptor
enclosure?" asked the first, leaning
forwards suspiciously. "Perhaps *you've*
got something to do with the raptors
not showing up to the games?"

Teggs groaned in despair. "We don't
have time for this!"

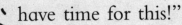

Outside, the
pterodactyls were still
zooming through the
air with their TV
cameras. The
commentator's voice
echoed from the stadium:
"*The tension mounts! In just a few
moments the great clock will chime . . .
and Hank and Crank will get butting!*"

"*Please!*" cried Gipsy. "We have to get out there and stop them!"

"Don't think so," snarled the second steward. "First, you have to get out of *here.*"

The five powerful predators advanced menacingly towards Teggs and Gipsy, drool dripping from their jaws . . .

Chapter Ten

DROPPING IN

"Sorry guys," said Teggs as he lashed
out at the nearest steward with his tail.
"But I think you'll thank me later!"
The carnotaurus was
knocked flying,
and the other
stewards leaped
back in surprise.
"Quick, Gipsy!"
he yelled. "Inside!"
    Together, they burst
into the royal paddock.
Close behind him came the
five stewards. Dinosaur kings and
queens gasped and shrieked as Teggs

and Gipsy pushed past them. They
spilled drinks, crushed crowns and sent
golden chairs scattering.

"Stop the contest!" Teggs yelled,
dodging the snapping jaws of the
nearest carnotaurus. "I'm a space
captain!"

"Look!" Gipsy cried.

She was staring in horror at an
enormous video screen.

The pterodactyls had zoomed in on the great clock. It was edging ever closer towards three. They only had seconds to stop Hank and Crank from making the biggest bang in dinosaur history!

Suddenly, Teggs had a brilliant idea.

"The pterodactyls, Gipsy!" he shouted, almost trampling several queens as he dodged another steward. "The ones with the TV cameras! Maybe they can lift us out into the stadium!"

"It's worth a try, sir!" Gipsy nimbly hopped onto the back of a startled diplodocus. Quickly, she whistled and clicked urgently at the flying reptiles high above them – just like she bossed about the dimorphodon on the *Sauropod's* flight deck.

Teggs backed away from the angry carnotaurus stewards who had finally fenced him in. They advanced, closer and closer, jaws snapping, little hands twitching . . .

Suddenly, a dozen pterodactyls dived out of the sky. They dropped the TV cameras on the stewards' heads, and sent them sprawling.

Teggs grinned at Gipsy. "I'm glad you speak fluent pterosaur!"

"I told them what I'd do to them if they didn't help!" Gipsy winked. "I'm just glad they believed me!"

Gipsy clicked and whistled some

91

more. A moment later, Teggs felt the armoured plates that ran down his back being gripped and lifted by twenty-four claws and twelve jaws.

The great clock chimed once. The sound was almost drowned out by the roar of the crowd.

"Quick!" yelled Teggs. Then his stumpy legs were kicking the air as he was lifted up, up into the sky.

The clock chimed twice.

Teggs gulped as he looked down. Gipsy was just a distant speck far below, but he thought he could hear her calling out. Wishing him luck.

"Good work, guys," he called to his flapping friends. He just hoped they spoke his language. "Now, see those orange nutters with the hard heads? Take me there!"

The clock chimed for the third and final time.

"Hurry!" Teggs bellowed.

As the crowd clapped and cheered, Hank and Crank ran out into the stadium.

"*Here we go, folks!*" the commentator cackled over the loudspeakers. "*These* hard-headed herbivores are ready for a bone-jarring skull-joust. I'm sure it'll be one we'll never forget!"

"Flap faster, fellas!" Teggs was almost directly above the athletes now . . .

Hank and Crank lowered their deadly heads. They were ready to charge . . .

"Right!" roared Teggs. "Put me down! Quick!"

But to his horror, the pterodactyls did *exactly* as he asked — and simply let go of him.

With a yell of surprise, Teggs began to plummet from the sky like a miniature meteor.

Beneath him, in the stadium, the stegoceras began to charge forwards.

"Stop!" Teggs cried desperately. "You mustn't hit your heads!"

Perhaps Hank and Crank couldn't hear him.

Perhaps they just weren't listening.

They ran on, faster and faster, the gap between them closing, *closing* . . .

95

And then the skydiving Teggs finally hit the ground — right between Hank and Crank! He gasped as the air was bashed from his body.

The shocked crowd fell utterly silent.

Hank and Crank were running too fast to stop. They crashed into Teggs's belly, then bounced backwards.

"Ooof!" grunted Teggs, as he screwed his eyes tightly shut. He waited for the inevitable blast of the bombs.

But nothing happened.

As he gingerly opened his eyes again, Teggs saw a worried hadrosaur bounding over to join him.

"Captain!" Gipsy cried. "Are you all right?"

"This must be how the meteor felt when it hit the Earth!" groaned Teggs weakly.

Gipsy hugged him. "I thought it was all over when Hank and Crank ran into you!"

"Must be that moss I scoffed before setting off," said Teggs. "Made my stomach extra springy and squashy – so the bombs didn't go off!"

As the coos and chatter of the startled crowd began again, Teggs heard two weak groans on either side of him.

"Hank!" he gasped. "Crank! Are you guys OK?"

"I never read anything about a flying stegosaurus in the rules," Hank muttered. "But it's a cool idea!"

"Yeah, awesome!" Crank agreed feebly. "But can someone please get this tail off my face?"

Teggs was about to oblige when a massive, menacing shadow fell over the stadium. It was pointed and curved like an enormous claw, scratching out the sun.

The crowd fell silent.

And Teggs and Gipsy found

themselves staring up at the sinister
shape of a massive raptor death ship.

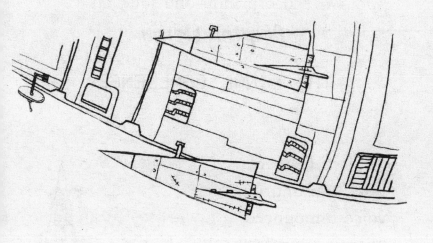

Chapter Eleven

THE FINAL CHALLENGE

"This is General Loki," an angry voice announced, booming out from the enormous spaceship. "I am Commander of the Seven Fleets of Death, ruler of the meat mines of Raptos, eater of— Well, you get the idea. Anyway – I bring an urgent message for Captain Teggs."

"Uh-oh," Teggs muttered. Gipsy tried to help him rise, but his legs were too bruised from the fall. He lay there helplessly, as if crushed into the ground by the weight of the ship's shadow.

"You've spoiled our evil plans, Captain," said Loki tetchily. "You've saved this entire, miserable planet from destruction."

A giant gasp went up from the crowd.

"Yes, I said *destruction*! If I had my way, you would all be space dust by now! But this pea-brained fool has spoiled all my plans—"

The crowd cheered and whooped.

"But you shall not enjoy your victory for long!" Loki added in his most sinister voice.

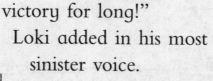

As the words echoed round the arena, a large cannon slid slowly out from underneath the raptor ship. It swivelled round until it was

aimed directly at Teggs. He and Gipsy
could only stare up at it helplessly.

But then another shadow fell. And
when Teggs saw what was casting it,
he grinned in amazement.

"This is the DSS *Sauropod*," Arx's voice
boomed out from the ship's speaker
system. "Perhaps you didn't hear,
General Loki? The raptors are a no-
show at this year's games — so get lost!"

With that, a volley of
laser fire tore loose
from the *Sauropod*.
As the red and
white lightning
burned and crackled
around the raptor
ship, the whole crowd
heard General Loki's howl of rage.

Then, with an ear-splitting sonic
boom, his death ship was sent spinning
away from the stadium. Soon, it had
vanished from view behind one of the
six scarlet suns glowing in the sky.

"We did it!" cried Gipsy, her crest
flushing bright red. "We saved the
planet!"

"*Ladies and gentlemen,*" announced the
bewildered commentator over the
speakers, "*it seems we owe a good deal
today to Captain Teggs — a truly amazing
astrosaur — and the crew of his fine ship, the
DSS Sauropod!*"

The crowd burst into thundering cheers and applause as the *Sauropod* flew slowly and gracefully off into orbit. Gipsy clapped too. Moments later, medics appeared. They swiftly tended to Teggs and the dazed athletes beside him.

As he was hefted away on a stretcher, Teggs smiled proudly up at the shrinking shape of his ship. He raised both his front legs in a dinosaur salute.

Some time later, Captain Teggs was back in his control pit, feasting on some of the finest ferns he had ever tasted. His legs felt much stronger, but he thought it best to take things easy for a while.

Beside him, Gipsy was busy reading aloud all the thank you messages they'd received.

"There's one here from Hank and Crank," she said happily. "The doctors have put their heads back to normal. But apparently they're really disappointed."

"Why?" wondered Teggs. "Because they couldn't take part in the games?"

"No," she chuckled. "Because they were hoping that exploding heads could become part of the sport!" She checked her read-out. "Hey, there's even a note from King Carnotaurus here. He says he's very sorry his stewards tried to eat you."

"No harm done," said Teggs briskly, turning to Arx. "Which I hope is more than can be said for General Loki?"

The triceratops smiled. "Iggy gave the lasers a power boost – enough to knock that raptor ship clear out of orbit! There's no telling where they'll end up!"

"Actually," said Iggy slyly, "there *is*." He gave Teggs a wicked grin. "I took a look with the long-range scanners, Captain. And guess what! Loki's ship will be forced to land for repairs somewhere around here . . ."

Iggy turned on the scanner with his stiff little tail and soon Teggs was staring at the green disc of a very familiar planet.

"Planet Sixty!" he beamed. "Really?"

"Serves them right," laughed Arx. "I wonder if that group of T. rexes is still there?"

Gipsy grinned. "They'll certainly keep Loki busy for a while!"

"And what about us?" asked Iggy. "I like to be kept busy too!"

"Take it easy while you can," came a booming voice. Everyone looked up to see a crusty old barosaurus on the scanner screen.

"Admiral Rosso!" gasped Gipsy.

"That's right!" he beamed. "I just

wanted to congratulate you all on
a job well done."

"Thank you, sir," said Teggs.

"Thank *you*," the admiral nodded.
"You've come through your first
mission with flying colours."

"And flying stegosaurs, too!"
whispered Gipsy, nudging Teggs in the
ribs.

"We couldn't have done it without
the *Sauropod*, sir," Teggs told him,
helping himself to an extra-big
mouthful of delicious ferns. "She's a fine
ship."

"And she has a fine crew," said the
admiral with a smile. "And you know
what? I have a hunch that somewhere
out there, a new adventure's waiting
. . . just around the corner."

Admiral Rosso's face faded from the
screen.

Now the scanner showed the view
outside the ship: the endless sparkle and

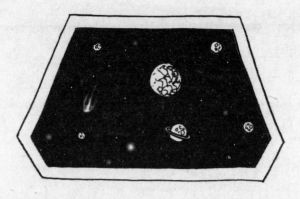

darkness of deep space. Teggs stared at it dreamily. He couldn't wait to explore it all.

"Well," he said. "I think we should get going."

Arx raised a bony eyebrow. "Where to, Captain?"

"You heard the admiral – just around the corner!" Teggs winked at him. "Don't you know it's rude to leave an adventure waiting?"

THE END

Chapter One

THE EDGE OF EGG-STINCTION!

In a very big hall full of very big dinosaurs, a very big announcement was about to be made.

The Hall of Learning on the planet Odo Minor had never been more packed. Doctors, professors, scientists, TV cameras – they were all squashed up together. The sound of excited dinosaur chatter filled the hall. What was the big news? What had the great Professor Sog discovered now?

But two people in the hall already knew. And one of them didn't seem to care very much.

"I don't see why we had to come all this way!" grumbled Captain Teggs Stegosaur. "I haven't been in a learning hall since I passed my astrosaur exams!"

"Be patient, Captain," his companion Gipsy hissed. "As soon as the talk's over, our mission can begin!"

"About time too," Teggs declared. He was a captain in the Dinosaur Space Service, and he lived for adventure. With his brave crew of astrosaurs, he travelled through space in the DSS *Sauropod*, the finest ship in the Jurassic Quadrant.

Gipsy, a stripy hadrosaur, was his communications officer. She and Teggs had come here to escort Professor Sog back to the *Sauropod* – along with some very special guests . . .

She knew her crewmates would be busy up in orbit. Arx Orano, Teggs's brainy triceratops first officer, would be checking over the *Sauropod*'s systems. And Iggy Tooth, the tough iguanodon engineer, would be stoking the ship's mighty engines.

Their latest voyage into outer space would be their longest yet ... .

"At last," cheered Teggs, making Gipsy jump. "Here comes Professor Sog now!"

Sog was a small, twittery old creature who belonged to a breed called compsognathus. The audience hooted and stamped their feet politely as the funny little figure walked onto the stage. He stopped beside a mysterious, lumpy bundle hidden beneath a black blanket.

A great hush fell on the hall. The dinosaurs waited breathlessly for the professor's words.

Sog struggled to put on a small pair of spectacles. He had trouble reaching his head since his arms were so short. But finally he managed it, and he peered round at the curious crowd.

"Welcome, my friends," he cried. "You are about to hear of a most exciting discovery!"

A bright light started glowing above his head. Seconds later, a hologram of a large, long-necked dinosaur appeared. It looked a bit like a stegosaurus but with a longer neck and tail, and no spiky plates running down its back.

"This is a plateosaurus," said Sog. "Sweet, peaceful — and almost totally extinct."

"Extinct?" asked a puzzled journalist in the crowd.

Sog nodded sadly. "Their race has almost completely died out."

"Dined out?" asked Teggs, perking up. He was famous for his large appetite — some said it was the largest in the whole Dinosaur Space Service. "Dined out where? Can we come too?"

"Not dined out, *died* out!" groaned Gipsy.

Professor Sog continued his talk. "As you all know, we dinosaurs left the Earth long ago. We escaped in spaceships before the meteor struck, never to return. In those days there were many plateosaurus. Nowadays there are hardly any left."

"Why?" someone called.

"Homesickness," said Sog simply. "At

first, they settled on a fine planet called Platus. But they didn't like it as much as Earth, so they tried to return." He shook his head sadly. "Their space fleet flew into a cosmic storm. Many of their ships were destroyed. The few survivors limped back to Platus . . . to find that T. rexes had taken over."

The audience murmured their disapproval.

"I remember reading about that," whispered Teggs. "The T. rexes wouldn't budge. There was a big battle."

Gipsy nodded sadly. "And the plateosaurus lost."

"Other vegetarian races came to their aid," the professor went on. "As you know, they joined together and formed the Dinosaur Space Service, to protect all plant-eaters. In the end they kicked the T. rexes off Platus. But the little planet had been almost ruined by war."

The hologram switched off above Sog's head. "The plateosaurus race never recovered from the tragedy. Today, only a tiny handful survive." He shuffled closer to the black bundle beside him. "But now I bring new hope!"

He clamped his jaws down on the blanket and whipped it away. Beneath

it was a pile of eight or nine large white eggs. The audience burst out in gasps and hoots. Flying reptiles flapped nearer with their

TV cameras to get a closer look.

"Plateosaurus eggs!" cried the little professor. "Discovered in a wrecked spaceship far out in the Jurassic Quadrant. That ship was a victim of the cosmic storm. It has drifted through space for thousands of years. But the eggs survived – frozen in space!"

The great hall filled with excited mutterings.

Professor Sog held up his feeble arms for quiet. "As you know, when it comes to hatching I am something of an expert . . ."

"*Eggs*-pert, more like!" Teggs chuckled.

"I was asked to study these old, old eggs," said Sog proudly. "And now that the eggs have thawed out, I believe that they will soon hatch! The plateosaurus race *will* live on!"

The audience cheered, and stamped their feet so hard that the floor shook.

"That's where we come in!" cried Teggs, rising to his feet. He flexed his long, bony tail, and knocked two elderly triceratops off their stools. "Oops!"

Sog frowned at the commotion. "Is that Captain Teggs?"

"Speaking!" he called cheerily, as Gipsy helped up the doddery dinosaurs. "Hello, everyone. It's my mission to take the professor, the eggs, and two plateosaurus guardians to a far-off world called Platus Two. A place where their race can make a fresh start!"

"*Is that a fact?!*"

Suddenly, the enormous wooden doors at the front of the hall were kicked open. The great hall rang with gasps of shock from the startled crowd.

Teggs narrowed his eyes. In the doorway stood a dozen small, ugly creatures. Their short, turtle-like heads bobbed about on scrawny necks.

One of the creatures darted towards the stage. "A fresh start for these lovely little hatchlings?" He shoved Professor Sog aside. "I don't think so! Not now the oviraptors are here!"

"Oviraptors?" frowned Teggs.

"Uh-oh!" Gipsy turned to Teggs in alarm. "They're nest-raiders! Egg-stealers!"

"We've got to stop them!" yelled Teggs. But he was blocked in on all sides by shocked old dinosaurs.

"I am Prince Goopo, and these are my royal brothers!" The oviraptor snatched up a plateosaurus egg and caressed it with his long, bony fingers. "Eggs are our favourite food, and eggs as rare as *these* will make a meal fit for a king – *and* his princes!" He threw back his head and laughed. "Forget your mission, Captain Teggs. The only place these eggs are going is *into our bellies!*"

Read the rest of
THE HATCHING HORROR
to find out if Teggs can
save the eggs!

Find your fantastic **ASTROSAURS** collector cards in the back of this book. More cards available in each **ASTROSAURS** title. You can also add to your collection by logging on to

www.astrosaurs.co.uk

TALKING DINOSAUR!

STEGOSAURUS –
STEG-oh-SORE-us

PTEROSAUR –
TEH-roh-sore

BAROSAURUS –
bar-oh-SORE-us

HADROSAUR –
HAD-roh-sore

TRICERATOPS –
try-SERRA-tops

IGUANODON –
ig-WA-noh-don

ORNITHOMIMOSAUR –
OR-ni-thoh-MEE-moh-sore

DIMORPHODON –
die-MORF-oh-don

VELOCIRAPTOR –
vel-ossi-RAP-tor

ANKYLOSAURUS –
an-KI-loh-SORE-us

SALTASAURUS –
sal-te-SORE-us

MAIASAURA –
MY-ah-SORE-ah

STEGOCERAS –
ste-GOS-er-as

EDMONTOSAURUS –
ed-MON-toh-SORE-us

DIPLODOCUS –
di-PLOH-do-kus

TYRANNOSAURUS –
tie-RAN-oh-SORE-us

CARNOTAURUS –
kar-noh-TOR-us

BRACHIOSAURUS –
brak-ee-oh-SORE-us

PTERODACTYL –
teh-roh-DACT-il

ASTROSAURS

BOOK TWO

THE HATCHING HORROR

Read the first chapter here!